Properties of Matter

Reflectiveness of Light

Arthur Best

New York

Published in 2019 by Cavendish Square Publishing, LLC
243 5th Avenue, Suite 136, New York, NY 10016

First Edition

Website: cavendishsq.com

Library of Congress Cataloging-in-Publication Data

Names: Best, B. J., 1976- author.
Title: Reflectiveness of light / Arthur Best.
Description: First edition. | New York : Cavendish Square, [2018] | Series: Properties of matter | Audience: K to grade 3. | Includes index.
Identifiers: LCCN 2018013849 (print) | LCCN 2018016092 (ebook) | ISBN 9781502642431 (ebook) |
ISBN 9781502642424 (library bound) | ISBN 9781502642400 (pbk.) | ISBN 9781502642417 (6 pack)
Subjects: LCSH: Reflection (Optics)--Juvenile literature. | Light--Properties--Juvenile literature.
Classification: LCC QC425.2 (ebook) | LCC QC425.2 .B47 2018 (print) | DDC 535/.323--dc23
LC record available at https://lccn.loc.gov/2018013849

Editorial Director: David McNamara
Copy Editor: Nathan Heidelberger
Associate Art Director: Alan Sliwinski
Designer: Megan Metté
Production Coordinator: Karol Szymczuk
Photo Research: J8 Media

The photographs in this book are used by permission and through the courtesy of: Cover Sakonboon Sansri/Shutterstock.com; p. 5 Billion Photos/Shutterstock.com; p. 7 Fenton/Shutterstock.com; p. 9 Megan Mette/Cavendish Square; p. 11 Fredy Jeanrenaud/iStockphoto.com; p. 13 Designua/Shutterstock.com; p. 15 Everything by EVE/Moment Open/Getty Images; p. 17 Alex Staroseltsev/Shutterstock.com; p. 19 Maks Narodenko/Shutterstock.com; p. 21 Mikhail Pankov/Alamy Stock Photo.

Printed in the United States of America

Contents

Light comes from
many places.

It comes from light bulbs.

It comes from the sun.

Light moves in **waves**.

The waves move back
and forth.

The waves are very small.

You can't see them.

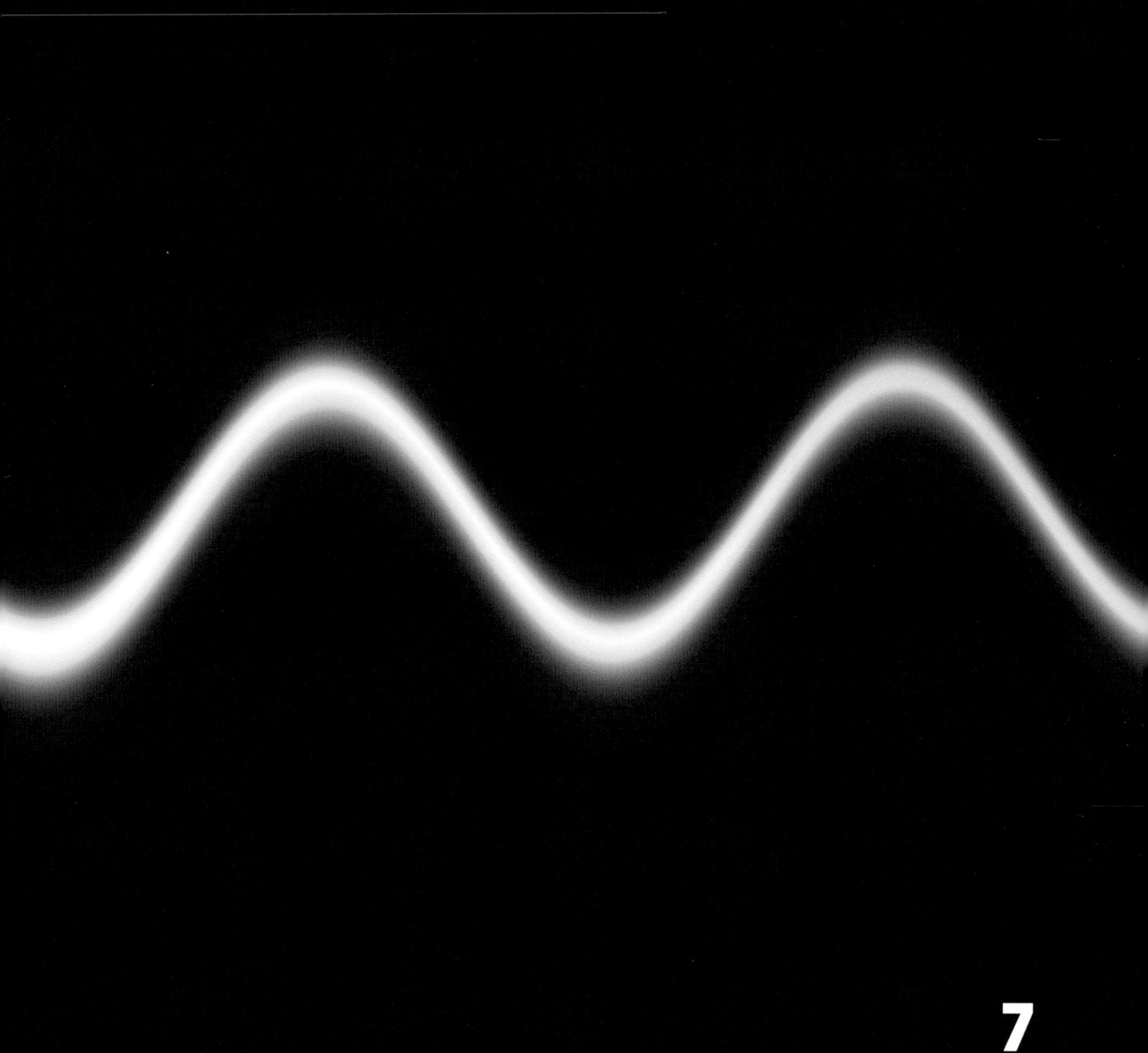

Light makes all colors.

Different waves make different colors.

Short waves of light make **violet**.

Long waves of light make red.

A rainbow shows all the colors in light.

Light from the sun goes through raindrops.

The light comes out in different waves.

The waves show all colors!

Things can **reflect** light.

Light hits something.

Then some light
bounces back.

This lets us see its color.

Rough things reflect less light.

Smooth things reflect more.

Mirrors reflect all light.

They are very smooth!

Here is an apple.

It is red.

It reflects long waves of light.

They are red.

It **absorbs** short waves.

Here is a pear.

It is green.

It reflects medium waves of light.

It absorbs short and long ones.

White things reflect all light.

Black things absorb all light.

Black things like roads get hot in the sun.

They get hot from the light they absorb!

New Words

absorbs (ab-ZORBZ) Soaks up.

reflect (re-FLEKT) Bounce back.

violet (VI-oh-let) Purple.

waves (WEYVZ) Things that move back and forth in patterns.

Index

About the Author

Arthur Best lives in Wisconsin with his wife and son. He has written many other books for children. He is somewhat bright.

About 

Bookworms help independent readers gain reading confidence through high-frequency words, simple sentences, and strong picture/text support. Each book explores a concept that helps children relate what they read to the world they live in.